PICK A CIRCLE, GATHER SQUARES
A FALL HARVEST OF SHAPES

Felicia Sanzari Chernesky

Illustrated by Susan Swan

Albert Whitman & Company
Chicago, Illinois

Library of Congress Cataloging-in-Publication Data

Chernesky, Felicia Sanzari.
Pick a circle, gather squares : a harvest of shapes / by Felicia Sanzari
Chernesky ; illustrated by Susan Swan.
pages cm
Summary: During a harvest hayride at Pumpkin Farm, a family finds
circles, squares, ovals, and other shapes all around.
[1. Stories in rhyme. 2. Shapes—Fiction. 3. Farm life—Fiction. 4.
Autumn—Fiction.] I. Swan, Susan, illustrator. II. Title.
PZ8.3.C4256Pic 2013
[E]—dc23
2013005186

Printed in China.
10 9 8 7 6 5 4 3 BP 18 17 16 15 14 13

For all the pumpkins
in my patch. —FSC

For Morgan, Kendall,
Roarke, Alex,
and Zane. —SS

Apple crisp October day.

Daddy says, "We're on our way."

Here we are, the pumpkin farm!
Next we'll travel arm in arm.

On our hayride to the patch
While we bump along we'll match
different shapes to what we see.
Will you harvest them with me?

Pick a **CIRCLE**!
Here's the sun.
Apples, pumpkins—
such **ROUND** fun!

Pluck a **SQUARE**! This bale of hay: a **CUBE** of straw's my seat today.

Gather **OVALS**! Squash and corn.
Speckled **EGGS** nest in the barn.

RECTANGLES?
A **BOX** of gourds,
big barn doors,
and wagon boards.

DIAMONDS darting in the sky
match the scarecrow's watchful eye.

HEXAGONS in honeycombs
and chicken wire where foxes roam.

See the fields? We're almost there.
Pumpkins, pumpkins everywhere!

Free
Hayride to
Pumpkin Patch

TRIANGLES make Daddy sigh
for a tasty **WEDGE** of pie.

Collect the **SHAPES**, and pumpkins, too.
Dad, I'll make a **HEART** for you!

Riding back we're seeing **STARS**:
stands with cider, mums, and jars.

Our harvest hayride helped us match so many **SHAPES**. Thanks, pumpkin patch!